Snow Bright
and the
Seven Sumos

Bill Condon

Illustrated by Ian Forss

SuPa
DOOPERS   sundance

Published by
Sundance Publishing
234 Taylor Street
Littleton, MA 01460

Copyright © text Bill Condon
Copyright © illustrations Ian Forss
Project commissioned and managed by
Lorraine Bambrough-Kelly, The Writer's Style
Designed by Cath Lindsey/design rescue

First published 1997 by
Addison Wesley Longman Australia Pty Limited
95 Coventry Street
South Melbourne 3205 Australia
Exclusive United States Distribution: Sundance Publishing

ISBN 0-7608-1927-0

Printed In Canada

Contents

To my friend Edel Wignel

CHAPTER 1
The Mean Queen

Twenty years ago, a nice girl named Jeannie journeyed to the kingdom of Boppityboo and entered the Boppityboo Smile Contest.

The best smilers from all over the world came to Boppityboo to compete for the first prize because it was big — very, very big. The winner of the contest won two tons of toothpaste, two hundred toothbrushes, a race car, a speedboat, a jet plane, AND she became the Queen of Boppityboo.

7

Twenty years ago, Jeannie's teeth shone so bright and pearly that the judges were almost blinded by their sparkling sheen.

No one had ever seen teeth so clean. They clapped and cheered and yelled, "What a grinner! She's the winner!"

So Jeannie became Queenie. Every year since, she has flashed her winning smile and won every Boppityboo Smile Contest with the greatest of ease.

But the fame and power and the millions that came with being the Queen of Boppityboo changed her.

She stopped being nice and became a
Mean Queen. Her smile turned into a nasty
snarl that scared snakes and bullied
bulldogs.

Despite this, she kept on winning the Boppityboo Smile Contest. Before each contest, she had the best artist in Boppityboo paint a brand-new smile on her face! No one was brave enough to tell her she was cheating.

"If I told the Queen she's cheating, she might cut off my head," said the village blacksmith. "That would make it very hard for me to eat my dinner."

CHAPTER 2

Chester the Jester

Feeling bored one day, the Queen called for her jester.

In a flash, Chester the Jester tumbled into the royal living room.

"What's 60 feet tall, weighs 50,000 pounds, and has two left feet?"

"I give up," replied the Queen.

"King Kong taking dancing lessons!" laughed Chester.

The Queen clicked her fingers. "Another riddle!"

"What sport do elephants play with snails?" he asked.

"Don't tell me," she said, "don't tell me . . . oh, all right, tell me."

"Squash!" yelled Chester, as he merrily danced around the room.

"Silence!" she snarled. "That's enough laughter for today."

Chester fell at the Queen's feet, almost too scared to breathe.

"Tell me what you know about this year's Boppityboo Smile Contest," she muttered.

"There are two thousand entries," he told her. "The most the contest has ever had."

"Not one of them can match . . . my supreme smile. Not one! Right?" she asked.

Chester hesitated. He didn't want to be the one to tell her the bad news.

She glared at him. "Do you have a secret, Jester?"

His teeth chattered, his knees knocked, and his ears wiggled.

"Out with it!" she screeched.

"I'm really sorry, Your Majesty," he whimpered, "but there *is* someone with a better smile than you."

She stomped and clomped around, shaking her head so hard it almost fell off. "That's impossible!" she roared. "You must be telling tales!"

"Oh, no, I'm not, Your Majesty. If you don't believe me, ask the magic mirror."

"I don't talk to mirrors!" yelled the Queen. "Do you think I'm crazy? Get out before I cut off your head!"

CHAPTER 3
The Magic Mirror

When Chester was gone, the Queen rushed to her drawer and took out her golden magic mirror.

She chanted:

Magic mirror, look at this smile,
Tell me it has lots of style.
Tell me it's the best you've seen,
Tell me that I'll long be Queen!

Dark clouds swirled in the mirror. Slowly, through the clouds, appeared two tiny lights. The lights grew until the Queen saw that they were eyes. Then there came a hairy nose and ears and a mouth — and finally the magic mirror spoke.

"Are you sure you want to know the truth?" it asked.

The Queen hurled the mirror to the floor and held her foot over it.

In her scariest voice, she hissed:

Mirror, mirror, don't mess around.
Who's got the cutest smile in town?
Is it me or is it not?
Give me the answer on the spot!

The mirror replied:

Oh, horrid Queen, you may turn green
and get a shocking fright
when the Smile Contest winner is…
announced as dear Snow Bright!

The Queen screamed. She hurled the
mirror back into the drawer and stomped
and clomped around.

CHAPTER 4
Sir Toby's Rotten Job

The Queen clanged her royal bell three times. In a flash her personal assistant, Sir Toby Toddle, came running.

She poked a bony finger at his nose. "What do you know about Snow Bright?"

Sir Toby rubbed his chin. "Hmm, not much, Your Majesty, except that she's very nice, she's smart, and she has a most gorgeous smile."

The Queen gasped, and then growled. "I want you to find her!"

"Would you like me to ask her to the palace for dinner?" Sir Toby asked.

"No, you silly sap!" the Queen shouted. "I want you to cut off her head!"

"B-b-b-but," he stammered, "if I cut off her head, her hat won't fit."

"That's right!" said the Queen. "And what's more, she won't win the Smile Contest, and I'll still be Queen of Boppityboo!"

Sir Toby pleaded with the Queen to show mercy, but she wouldn't listen.

"You have until tonight to get rid of Snow Bright, or I'll get rid of you!" she threatened.

"Ah, well, that's different," he said. "Never fear, Your Majesty. I'll wipe that smile off Snow Bright's face!"

CHAPTER 5

Heading for Trouble

Snow Bright had just brushed each tooth one hundred times. "I wish someone would come along so I could practice my smile," she said.

At that moment Sir Toby Toddle knocked on her door. "Come out, Snow Bright," he called. "There's no use trying to hide."

"Why would I hide?" she asked, as she opened the door.

Sir Toby lifted a huge ax above her head.

Snow Bright gave him her most dazzling smile.

"Oh, thank you very much, but I don't need a haircut today."

"What a cool smile you have," he remarked.

"How clever of you to notice."

No one had ever thought Sir Toby was clever. He was so shocked that he dropped the ax on his big toe. It hurt so much that he blurted out a very rude word.

The very rude word made Snow Bright giggle. And before long Sir Toby began to giggle, too.

When they stopped giggling, she poured him a cold drink and put a bandage on his toe.

"I was supposed to cut off your head," he explained. "But you're much too nice for that."

"That's just as well," said Snow Bright. "I'd look silly without a head."

Sir Toby spared Snow Bright's life, but only after making her promise not to enter the Smile Contest.

"You also must go into hiding for the rest of your life," he warned. "If the Queen finds out you're alive, she'll kill us both."

Snow Bright agreed, and the two parted as friends.

CHAPTER 6

Snow Bright Meets
the Sumos

Snow Bright moved into a cave and found
a job in a baked bean factory. She kept to
herself and never ever smiled.

One day, seven singing sumo wrestlers —
Frisky, Frosty, Floppy, Flippy, Fizzy, Fuzzy,
and George — came to the factory to buy
seven hundred cans of baked beans. This
was just enough to last them seven weeks.

They were the first singing sumo wrestlers
Snow Bright had ever heard.

Hi ho, hi ho, we're wrest-a-ling sumo.
We'll fight tonight with all our might,
Hi ho, hi ho, hi ho!

Before she could stop herself, a gleaming smile appeared on Snow Bright's face.

"Your smile's wicked cool!" they said.

"I'm Snow Bright," she said. "But you mustn't tell anyone about me, or my smile."

"Why not?" asked George.

And so Snow Bright told the sumos her tale.

"That's the saddest story I've ever heard," Fuzzy said. "Come and live with us. We'll protect you from the Queen."

"We will be your very best friends," Flippy added.

"Oh, thank you so much," Snow Bright replied. "In return, I'll cook for you."

The sumos jumped for joy. The only thing *they* could cook was baked beans.

"With more good food, we might start winning our wrestling matches," Floppy grinned.

Snow Bright felt his arm, but she couldn't find any muscles. "You need a trainer as well as a cook," she said.

"We can't afford a trainer," Frosty muttered.

Beaming her most brilliant smile, Snow Bright declared, "I will be your cook *and* your trainer!"

"Hurray!" shouted the sumos.

CHAPTER 7

The Truth Comes Out

With Snow Bright out of the way, the Mean Queen easily won the Boppityboo Smile Contest.

For a while, she was happy and hardly cut off any heads. But then she began hearing stories about a beautiful sumo wrestler trainer.

The villagers had seen her at matches, cheering for her seven wrestlers. And they remembered her because of her wonderful smile.

"It's a razzle-dazzle smile!" they said. "The best smile in all of Boppityboo!"

The Queen grabbed her magic mirror and chanted:

Magic mirror, look at this smile,
Tell me it has winning style.
Tell me it's the best you've seen,
Tell me that I'll long be Queen!

Once more, dark clouds swirled in the mirror. Soon there were two tiny lights that became eyes, then she saw a hairy nose and ears and a mouth — and finally the magic mirror spoke.

I promise you that I am right,
Another's smile is much more bright.

The Queen's eyes blazed with anger. "Who is it? Who dares to better my smile?"

"Snow Bright," the mirror answered.

The Queen shouted:

> *Mirror, mirror, use your head —*
> *that can't be right*
> *'cause Snowie's dead!*

> *"Sorry," said the mirror,*
> *"she's not in heaven,*
> *she's working for the sumo seven!"*

"Curses!" howled the Queen. "This time I'll kill Snow Bright myself!"

CHAPTER 8
The Poison Soup

Far away in the hills, a party was being held. The sumos had never been so happy, for they had each won a medal at the Boppityboo Games.

"It was your good training and cooking that made us winners," Frisky told Snow Bright.

The others gave her three hearty cheers and a present they had made themselves — a double-layer baked bean cake.

"It's scrumptious!" she exclaimed.

The sumos laughed and danced until it was time for them to leave for their jobs as fishermen.

As they strolled to their boats, they sang this song:

Hi ho, hi ho, to catch some fish we go,
We'll fish all night with all our might,
Hi ho, hi ho, hi ho!

Soon afterward, someone knocked on the door. Peeping through a curtain, Snow Bright saw an old lady. She did not know that the old lady was the Mean Queen in disguise.

Snow Bright opened the door and the Queen said, "I made some mushroom soup, just for you."

"How kind!" said Snow Bright.

She took a little sip of soup. Then a big slurp. "Yum-yum!" she declared. "It's delicious!"

The Queen could hardly believe it. "Let me taste it!" she said.

She grabbed the bowl and swallowed a super slurp of soup. Then another and another! Then she turned green—a mean green Queen who started to lean and lean and lean—and CRASH!

"Oh, my goodness!" exclaimed Snow Bright. "She's deadybones. I wonder if there was something wrong with the soup?"

The next second, she found out the terrible truth. CRASH! Snow Bright was down and out, too.

CHAPTER 9
A Sleeping Beauty

The nasty Mean Queen had drunk so much poison mushroom soup that she was definitely deadybones. Fortunately, Snow Bright hadn't drunk as much, so she was alive, but only just barely. The poison had caused her to fall into a deep sleep.

"We'll get the best doctors in the kingdom," said Frosty. "They'll wake her!"

One by one, the doctors came. There were doctors for:
>the heart,
>the kidneys,
>the lungs,
>and the liver.
>AND
>there was even a mushroom soup specialist!

But no one could wake her.

The sumos stayed with her day and night, telling her jokes and singing her favorite songs. But Snow Bright still didn't wake up.

When all hope was almost lost, a handsome young man named Princeton arrived at the sumos' home. He'd heard of Snow Bright's smile, and he wanted her to star in his new toothpaste commercial.

The sumos were so sad.

"What's wrong?" Princeton asked.

"You're too late," Fuzzy said. "Look." He pointed to the bedroom where Snow Bright slept.

Wiping their eyes while standing around Snow Bright's bed, the sumos told him what had happened.

"Gee, that's a shame," Princeton replied. "I wish I could do something to help."

"No one can help," muttered George.

As Princeton was about to leave, he bent down and gave Snow Bright a kiss for luck.

Suddenly her eyes popped open.

"What an awful smell!" she cried.

"Sorry," said Princeton. "I just ate a garlic pizza."

The sumos whooped with joy. "She's awake! Our lovely Snow Bright is awake!"

CHAPTER 10

A Happy Ending

Shortly afterward, the annual Boppityboo
Smile Contest was held. It came as no
surprise when Snow Bright was declared
the winner.

She won:
>   two tons of toothpaste,
>   two hundred toothbrushes,
>   a race car,
>   a speedboat,
>   and a jet plane.
>   AND
>   she became the Queen of Boppityboo!

The new Queen was never mean. The kingdom was a happy one, and no more heads were cut off in Boppityboo.

With Sir Toby Toddle as their trainer, the seven sumo wrestlers became world champions.

And the Queen gave Chester the Jester some money to buy new jokes.

But what happened to Princeton, the charming man whose smelly kiss saved Snow Bright?

He now has shortened his name to Prince, and the Queen calls him Prince Charming. They make a lovely couple. Every time they see each other, they can't help smiling.

Today, wherever you go in Boppityboo, you will hear the national anthem sung. It sounds just like this:

Hi ho, hi ho, a'smiling we will go,
We'll smile and smile like a crocodile,
Hi ho, hi ho, hi ho!

About the Author

Bill Condon

Bill Condon was one of Australia's leading sumo wrestlers before his terrible accident — he belly-flopped onto a trampoline and all his fat shifted downward. Now he sits in a very wide chair writing funny stories. He lives in Sydney, Australia, and has had about forty children's books published.

About the Illustrator

Ian Forss

In 1969, when Ian Forss was nine years old, his mother commented that a picture he had drawn looked "nice." That was all the encouragement he needed. From then on he was always to be found drawing pictures.

Ian drew all the way through college as he earned a degree in Art and Design. And when he went on to earn a graduate degree in Film and Television, he was still drawing.

Today, Ian lives with his wife, Linda, and two children, Jade and James. He enjoys riding his horse, Apache, even if sometimes it makes drawing steady lines a bit tricky.